SLAM!™

THE NEXT JAM

BOOM! BOX

BOOM! Studios, 5670 Wilshire Boulevard, Suite 400, Los Angeles, CA 90036-5679. Printed in China. First Printing.

ISBN: 978-1-68415-120-2, eISBN: 978-1-61398-859-6

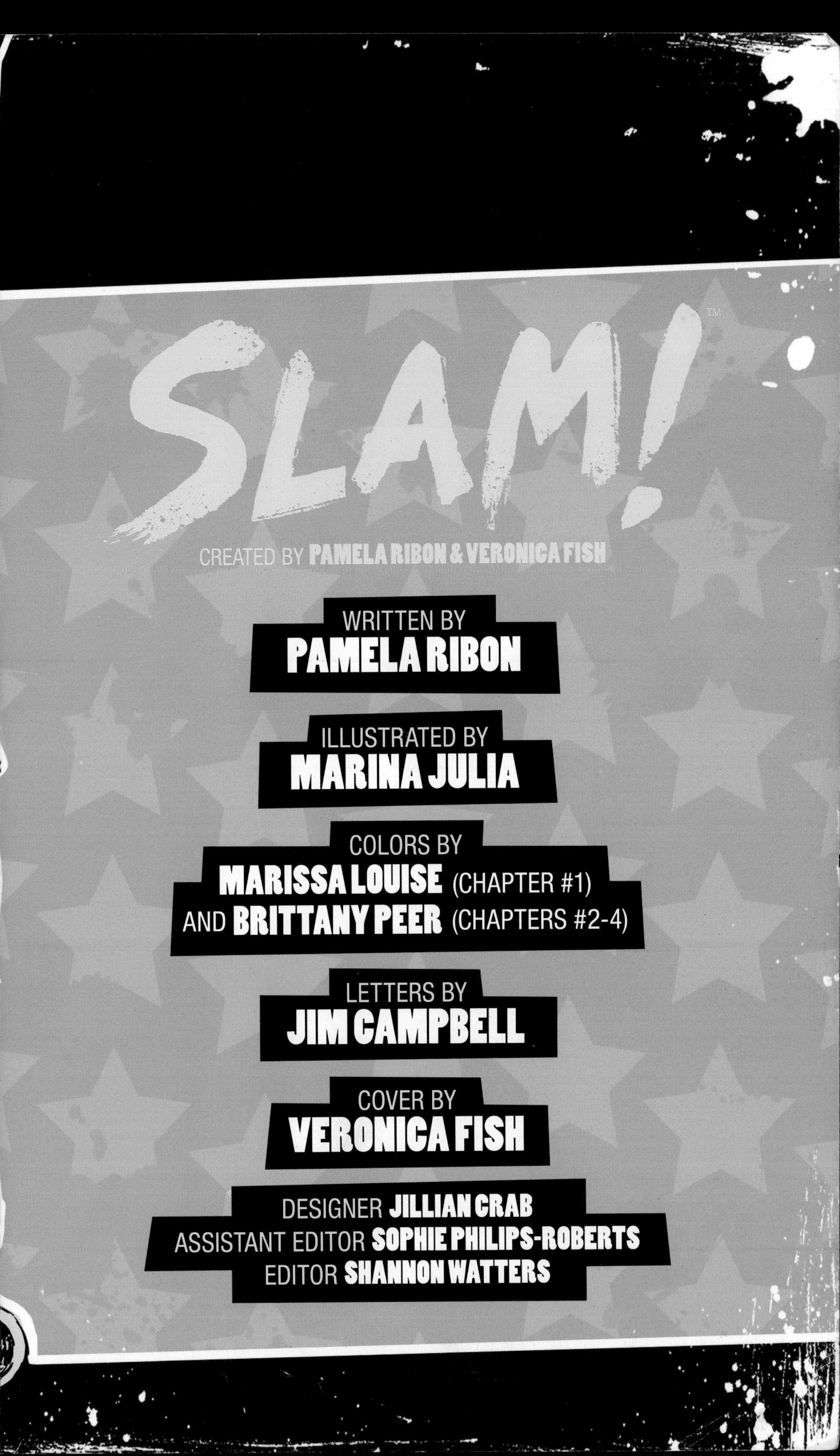

SLAM!™

CREATED BY **PAMELA RIBON & VERONICA FISH**

WRITTEN BY
PAMELA RIBON

ILLUSTRATED BY
MARINA JULIA

COLORS BY
MARISSA LOUISE (CHAPTER #1)
AND **BRITTANY PEER** (CHAPTERS #2-4)

LETTERS BY
JIM CAMPBELL

COVER BY
VERONICA FISH

DESIGNER **JILLIAN CRAB**
ASSISTANT EDITOR **SOPHIE PHILIPS-ROBERTS**
EDITOR **SHANNON WATTERS**

CHAPTER ONE

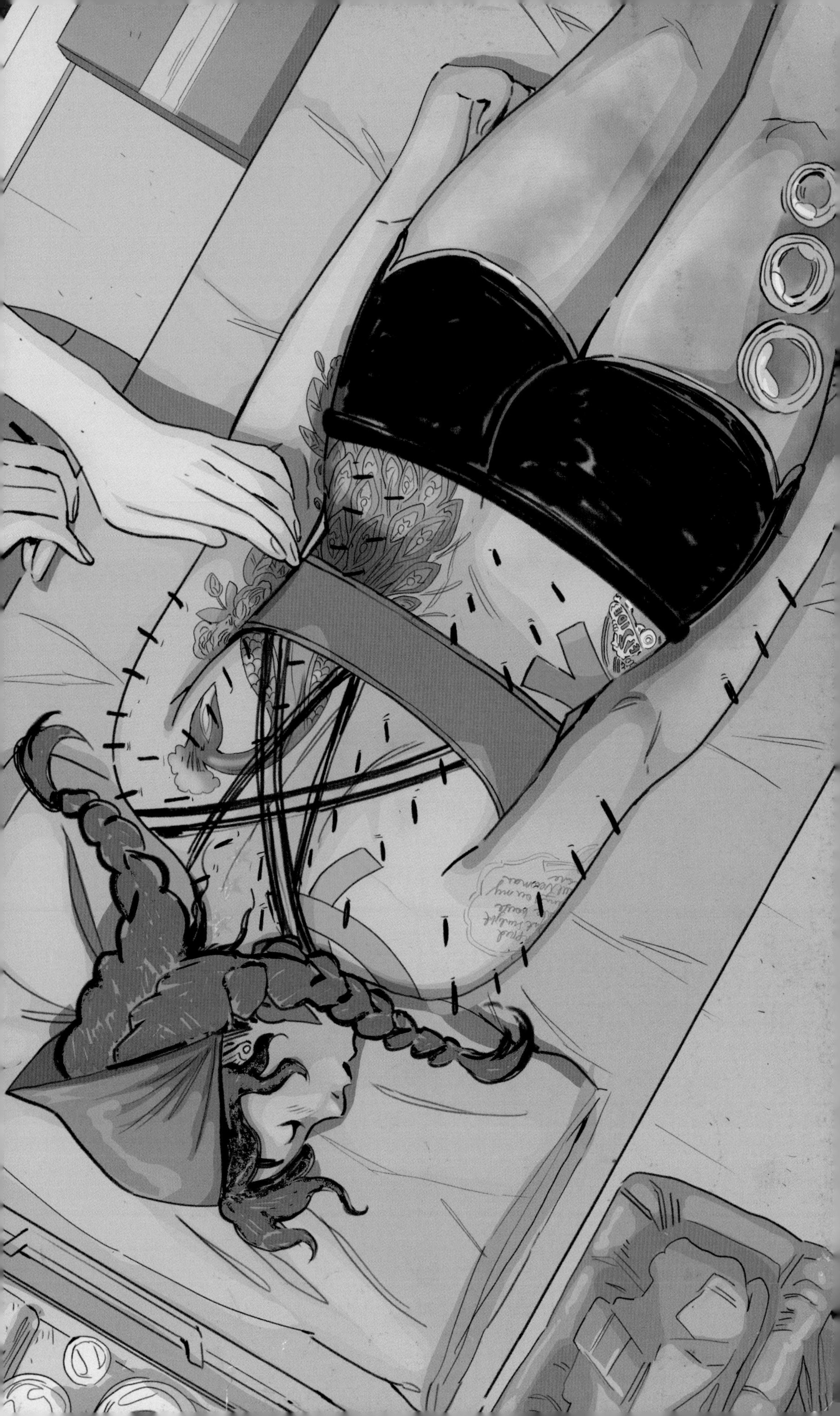

FRIDAY, 8PM.
EAST SIDE ROLLER GIRLS UTILITY/OFFICE/CONFERENCE ROOM.
ART DEPARTMEN MEETING.
WE STILL NEED ART FOR THE ROOKIE RUMBLE PROMO.
I THOUGHT WE'D WAIT UNTIL THEY HAVE TEAMS. SHOULD BE NEXT WEEK.
I ORDERED MORE FLYERS FOR CHAMPS.
RIOTS
VS
SATURDAY
8PM
EAST SIDE ROLLER GIRLS
I'M TEMPTED TO PUT AN ASTERISK RIGHT OVER KNOCKOUT'S FACE, SINCE SHE WON'T BE SKATING.

I THINK IT'S COOL, WHAT SHE DID. I DON'T GET WHY PEOPLE ARE SO UPSET.
CANCAN'S HER BEST FRIEND. SHE WAS REALLY HURT.
WE ALL GET REALLY HURT.
YOU DON'T DITCH YOUR TEAM DURING A BOUT. IF I RAN THE PUSHY RIOTS, I'D BOOT HER PERMANENTLY.
I MEAN, THEY MIGHT. WITH CANCAN I--
CANCAN
I NEED SWIFFERS AND LYSOL.
COOL.
DERBY LIFE LESSON #12 (...AND 13, 117 & 143): DERBY DRAMA IS THE WORST.

HERE, I GOT IT.
THANKS, KRISTEN.
HEY, DO YOU THINK YOU COULD GIVE ME A RIDE HOME AFTER WE'RE DONE?
HUH? NO, I CAN'T DRIVE.
ARE YOU EXCITED ABOUT THE ROOKIE RUMBLE? YOU SIGNED UP, RIGHT?
YES. I CAN'T WAIT TO HUMILIATE MYSELF IN FRONT OF EVERY TEAM SKATER ON HIATUS.
YOU'LL BE GREAT.
YOU AND KNOCKOUT GOT DRAFTED AFTER YOUR ROOKIE RUMBLE, RIGHT?
YEAH...

"... SHE WAS THE NUMBER ONE PICK."
EASTSIDE ROLLERS GIRLS

ANY WORD?
NOPE.

THEY'RE LETTING ME SWEAT IT OUT.
BUT I KEEP COMING TO PRACTICE. GETTING MY ATTENDANCE HOURS.
I'M STILL ON THIS TEAM.
I SHOULD PROBABLY LEAVE YOU ALONE.
DON'T. I WOULD JUMP THAT TRACK FOR YOU AGAIN TOMORROW.
IF THEY DON'T LIKE THAT ABOUT ME, THEY SHOULD CUT ME.
KNOCKOUT, CAN I GET A RIDE HOME?

I'LL SEND YOU SOME GAS MONEY AS SOON AS I CHARGE MY PHONE.
THANKS.
YOU LIVE LIKE HALF A MILE FROM THE TRACK. IT'S FINE. BE SAFE.
DID YOU REMEMBER LAUNDRY DETERGENT?
YEP.
THIS IS NICE. YOU AREN'T AS STINKY AS USUAL.
DON'T GET USED TO IT.
HOW IS SHE?
ASLEEP, I HOPE.

EITHER KILL ME OR LET ME SLEEP, INTRUDER.
RECORD TRACK
BASKETBALL

YOU SAW THE ARNICA I LEFT ON THE COUNTER?
YES, THANKS.
OW.

SATURDAY, 8 AM.
METEORFIGHTS OFF-SKATES EXTRA PRIVATE PRACTICE.
WE'RE TAKING OUR OFF-SEASON TRAINING SERIOUSLY THIS YEAR.
I PLAN ON SKATING THE EXPO BOUT NEXT MONTH.
THAT SEEMS... SOON.
WHEN YOU WERE OUT WITH YOUR ARM--
A QUICK TWO MILES AND THEN IT'S MIMOSAS, MF'ERS!
SORRY, GOTTA--
OH, SURE, YEAH, BYE, BROKE-BROKE. SEE YA ON THE FLIP.
...I GUESS I'M A PERSON WHO SAYS 'ON THE FLIP' NOW.
YOU CAN BE COMPLETELY SURROUNDED BY DERBY DRAMA AND STILL FIND YOURSELF ALL ALONE.

SUNDAY, 8 PM.
FRESH MEAT SCRIMMAGE.
MMMFFMRUFPH!
JAMMER UP HIGH! JAMMER UP HIGH!
I GOT HER!
HIT HIGH, HIT HIGH!
GET OUT OF THERE, KRISTEN! GET OUT! GET OUT!

NEXT PACK! SARAH, GUAD, PATTY--
I CAN'T. I'M TOAST.
I'LL GO AGAIN.
YES!
YAY!

GOOD JOB TONIGHT!
YEAH, GREAT WORK.
BYE, KRISTEN! WE LOVE YOU!
THANKS, LADIES.

HEY, LĀOLAO. I BROUGHT THAT PHONE CHARGER FOR MOMMY.
YOU DON'T NEED TO TELL ME YOUR EVERY MINUTE. I AM NOT AN APP.
YOU HEARD THEY'RE CUTTING ME UP AGAIN?
YES. WHAT ARE THEY DOING TO YOUR FOOT THIS TIME?
I DON'T KNOW. IT'S NONE OF MY BUSINESS.
CAREFUL. THOSE EXERCISES WILL GIVE YOU A BIG BUTT.
TOO LATE.
WHO IS LOVING YOU THESE DAYS?
WELL, GOTTA GO.

ALOOOOOOOONE!
AAAALOOOOOOOOOOONE!
SATURDAY, 5:30 PM.
BOUT DAY. CHAMPS.
GOOD LUCK.
THANKS.
EASTSIDE
YOU HAVE TO CLEAN THE BATHROOM. WE LEFT A LITTLE MESS IN THERE GETTING READY.
'KAY.

RRGH.
HI! WELCOME TO THE EAST SIDE ROLLER GIRLS! IS THIS YOUR FIRST TIME?
BOTH PUSHY RIOTS AND THE FURIOSAS ARE ON THE TRACK AND WARMING UP.
MAYBE THIS ISN'T THE JOB FOR YOU.
CHAMPS START IN LESS THAN TEN MINUTES!

THE PUSHIES WILL HAVE TO WORK EXTRA HARD TO MAKE UP FOR THEIR MISSING--
--TEAMMATE KNOCKOUT, WHO'S CURRENTLY ON PROBATION PENDING A DECISION FROM--
TWEET
THE ENTIRE SPORT IS ABOUT HOW YOU RESPOND TO A HIT.
HOW COULD THERE NOT BE DRAMA?
FURIOSAS! YES! YES!
YOU!
LAS FURIOSAS

I'M GONNA MARRY THAT GIRL.
YOU'RE WRATHKO, RIGHT? AREN'T YOU AN *NSO?**
YEAH, BUT TONIGHT I WANTED TO DRINK AND SCREAM MY HEAD OFF.
*NSO: NON-SKATING OFFICIAL.
YOU'RE WITH CANCAN, YEAH?
YEAH. I'M THEO. THE PUSHIES ARE FIGHTING HARD.
VELVET IS A MACHINE. BUT THE FURIES REALLY WANT THIS.
THEY'VE NEVER COME THIS CLOSE TO CHAMPS BEFORE. THEY WORKED THEIR ASSES OFF.
AND THANKS TO YOUR GIRL'S TUMBLE, THEY MIGHT WIN.
DO YOU THINK KNOCKOUT WILL BE KICKED OFF THE TEAM?
OR THE WHOLE LEAGUE?
SHE'D GET RECRUITED SOMEWHERE ELSE IN A HEARTBEAT.
I'M RED. RED KENNEDY. I JUST TRANSFERRED HERE.

PUSHY RIOTS
VS
LAS FURIOSAS
101
TIMEOUTS
2
2
108

WHAT ARE YOU...?
PLEASE JUST LET ME BE HELPFUL.
I HAVE TO CLEAN STORAGE NEXT.
PUSHIES TIE IT AGAIN! ONE-TEN TO ONE-TEN!
...AND VELVET COFFIN IS EJECTED FOR PENALTIES!
AFTER SUCH A LONG UNDEFEATED STREAK, THIS IS A REAL BLOW TO THE PUSHY RIOTS.
THE THING IS, EVEN IF YOU TRY YOUR VERY BEST TO KEEP YOUR HEAD DOWN TO AVOID IT...

LAS FURIOSAS
...DERBY DRAMA'S GONNA FIND YOU.
YOU!
THIS IS HUGE.
TUESDAY NIGHT. AFTER THE LEAGUE MEETING. WE'LL GIVE YOU OUR DECISION.
HEY, CAN I GET A RIDE HOME?

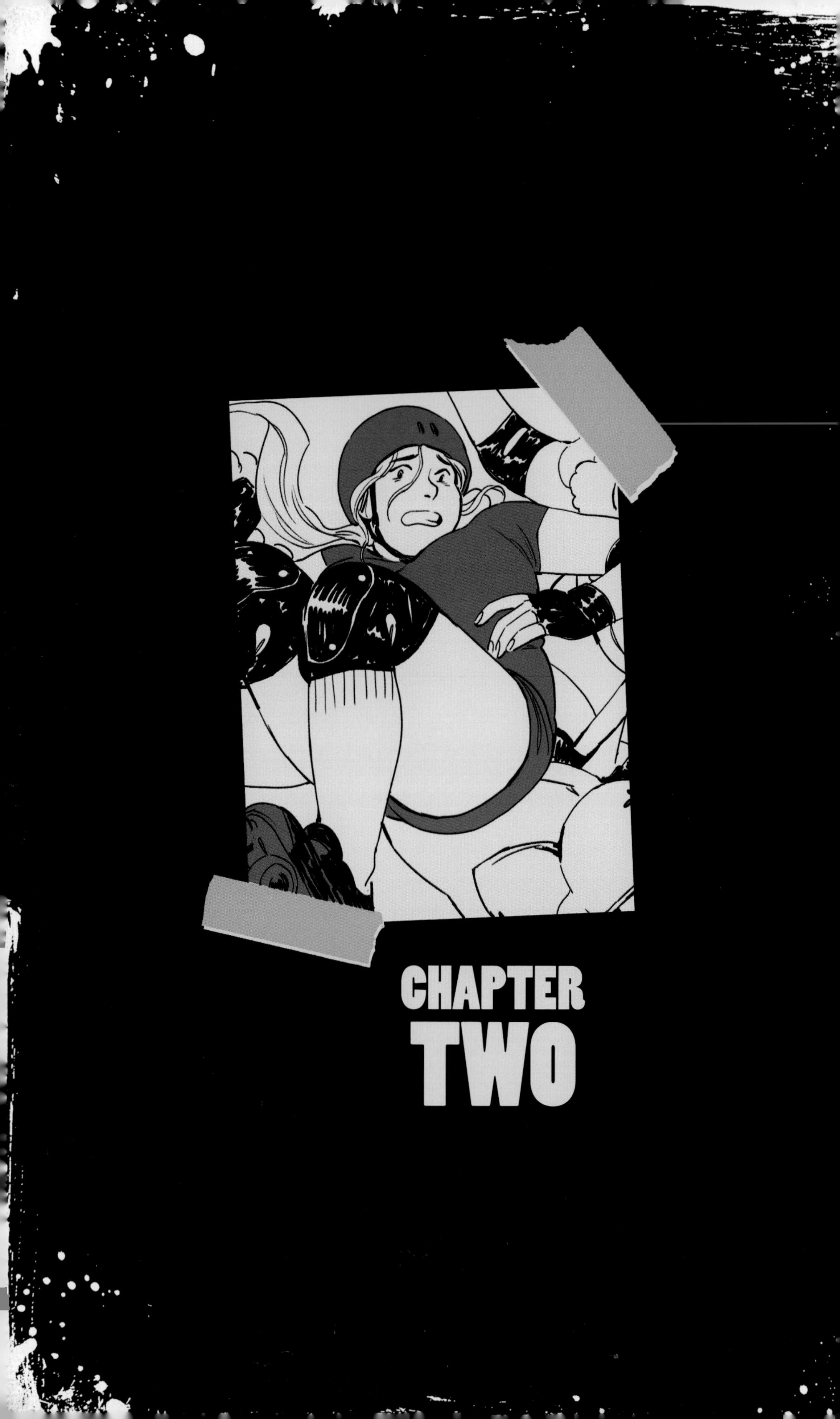

CHAPTER TWO

OKAY, FRESHIES!
TIME FOR MY FAVORITE GAME!
LAST GIRL STANDING!
Scaredy Kat

OOF!
DERBY FACT #26: THERE IS NO "EASY WAY" TO GET THROUGH FRESH MEAT.
EVERYONE HITS A PERSONAL ROCK BOTTOM.
OW. OW. OW.
BUT NOT EVERYONE WILL GET BACK UP.
OH, GOD...
OOOKAY, THAT'S A WRAP ON ME AND DERBY.
I LOVE THIS SPORT WITH EVERY FIBER OF MY BEING.

HA! YOU MISSED!
SWOOOOSH
BECAUSE SOMETIMES IT'S NOT ABOUT WHAT'S KNOCKING YOU DOWN.
THWAK
KRISTEN! YOU CAN'T JUST RUN AWAY FROM HER!
WATCH ME!
IT'S ABOUT WHAT'S CHASING YOU.

MEANWHILE, AT THE PUSHY RIOTS PRIVATE MEETING...
I WILL TALLY THESE VOTES AND THE VERDICT WILL BECOME LAW.
YOU GUYS KNOW I'M NOT ON ACTUAL TRIAL, RIGHT?
NOBODY HERE HAS A LAW DEGREE.

ACTUALLY, STARBUCKER'S A PUBLIC DEFENDER.
I COUNSEL YOU TO SHUT IT.
MAKE THEM SHUT UP OUT THERE.
BANG
BANG
BANG
BANG

OW.
HOW MUCH LONGER CAN THIS GO ON?
SHE'S GOING TO BE FINE.
ARE YOU SURE?
MOSTLY.
WHAT ARE THOSE GUYS TALKING ABOUT?
YOU SAW THE ROOKIE RUMBLE PROMO?
ESRG ★ Aug 7th
WHISTLE @ 8

GO BABY, GO!
ROOKIE RUMBLE!
ESRG ★ Aug 7th
DOORS @ 6
WHISTLE @ 8
YOU DON'T THINK IT'S CUTE?
THE ARGUMENT CAN BE MADE THAT THERE'S ZERO POINT ZERO ROLLER DERBY IN THAT PROMO.

BANG
OW.
WE CAN'T KEEP PLAYING IF WE DON'T HAVE ANYONE IN THE SEATS.
SO WE HAVE TO SEXUALIZE OURSELVES IN ORDER TO SKATE?
IT'S JUST SUPPOSED TO BE FUNNY.
I HAVE OVER TEN THOUSAND DOLLARS IN UNPAID MEDICAL BILLS, AND SEVERAL PINS AND RODS PERMANENTLY INSIDE MY BODY. I SHOULDN'T HAVE TO VOLUNTEER THE OPPORTUNITY TO SEE MY ASS CRACK TO--
QUIET!
THEY'RE SAYING SOMETHING!
I CAN'T... QUITE...
ONE MONTH PROBATION AFTER HIATUS WITH MANDATORY COACHING OF A ROOKIE RUMBLE TEAM.
SEE? NOT KICKED OFF.
BUT SHE DOESN'T HAVE TIME TO COACH! HER--

--GRANDMOTHER'S NOT WELL. I'M SUPPOSED TO--
DO YOU KNOW I WAS IN FRESH MEAT FOR FIVE YEARS?
FIVE. YEARS.
IF YOU SUCKED AT SKATING, YOU WOULD HAVE BEEN GONE. THINK OF ALL THE SKATERS WHO WOULD DO ANYTHING TO BE WHERE YOU ARE. SHOW SOME GRATITUDE.

GO BABY, GO! ROOKIE RUMBLE

ROOKIE RUMBLE TEAM A, FIRST PRACTICE.
OKAY, MEATIES! LET'S SEE WHAT YOU'VE GOT!
TWEET!
THWAK
CRSH
WHAM
THUD

DID YOU HEAR OUR PRIVATE HOURS DON'T COUNT TOWARD ATTENDANCE? THAT SUCKS.
WE'RE *REAL* BAD.

YIKES ON ALL THIS I'M SEEING.
ME TOO, BUT OVER HERE.
CAMILLA
ANGIE
I HATE THIS!
DIGNITY SHORTS
GET A NEW POSTER
I HATE THIS POSTER
ESR6 * AUG 7TH
DOORS @6 WHISTLE @8
REF INTRO CLASS
I SMELL PIZZA!
TWEET TWEET TWEET
OKAY, FRESHIES! PACE LINE NOW! NOW! NOW!

HUSTLE, HUSTLE!
MOVE IT- MOVE IT!
GET UP!
WHAT IS WRONG WITH YOU?
HIT HER!
STOP! STOP!
GO! GO!
FASTER!
NO! NO! WHY?
THAT'S NOT WHAT SKATING LOOKS LIKE!

MEANWHILE...
PKAWK!
HA-HA-HA-- THAT IS NOT WHAT AN EAGLE SOUNDS LIKE!
I PANICKED!
METEORFIGHTS BONDING NIGHT, KIM BIGDEAL'S APARTMENT.
OCELOT!
WHAT?!

HEY, GAL? ARE YOU MAD AT ME?
NO. YOU SCARE ME.
YOU REMIND ME HOW EASILY I COULD BE BROKEN AGAIN.
AND I FULLY KNOW THAT MAKES ME A HORRIBLE PERSON.
I'M SORRY.
NICE BUTT BRUISE, BIGDEAL!
SEVEN POINT EIGHT!
YOU LIKE IT? YOU LIKE THIS?
SKATERS? PLEASE BRING YOUR SCARS TO THE RUNWAY!

I NAMED HER MILLIE, SHORT FOR MILLIPEDE.
WHY, THANK YOU, YES. I'M WEARING PERMANENT WHIPLASH, SCIATICA, AND A RECENT HIP SURGERY!
DISTH TOOFTH ITH FAKE!
ALWAITH WEAR YOUR MOUTHGUARD, KIDTH!
WE ARE WOMEN WHO DELIVERED VAGINALLY!
SOMETIMES WHEN YOU HIT US, WE PEE!
URINE TROUBLE WITH US!

I CAN'T COMPETE WITH THE MAGICAL VAGINALS!
I CAN'T WAIT TO FIND OUT WHEN THIS WILL BE FUNNY.
MFF.
IT'S OKAY, CANCAN.
WE GOT YOU, HON.
AW, HER POOR WING.
WATCH HER ARM.

HEY! I DIDN'T KNOW YOU WERE COMING OVER TONIGHT.
I TEXTED YOU A FEW TIMES.
SORRY. MY PHONE DIED AND I WAS IN THE POOL.
GOOD NIGHT?
YES.
ME TOO.
GREAT.
INCOMING:
U up?
Knockout:
y
INCOMING:
open ur door

I GOT AN UBER, I COULDN'T SLEEP.
I'M BUSY.
I KNOW.
BUT LISTEN.
YOU'RE SCARY.
WHAT?
DO YOU HAVE A MIRROR? YOU SHOULD SEE THIS.
WHY BE SO YELLY AND SAY MEAN THINGS AND BLOW THE WHISTLE SO HARD?
I WAS *COACHING!* AND BLOWING WHISTLES IS HOW YOU MAKE THEM WORK.

REALLY? BECAUSE I THINK YOU COULD BE LESS OF A... *BLOW-HARD.*
SNICKER
WHAT ARE YOU DOING HERE?
IT'S MIDNIGHT. THIS ISN'T CUTE. YOU'RE NOT CUTE.
FIXING YOUR FROWN.
PIZZA
MIDNIGHT, *HUH?*
SORRY. DIDN'T KNOW OUR RELATIONSHIP HAD LIKE, A *CURFEW.*
"... *RELATIONSHIP?*"

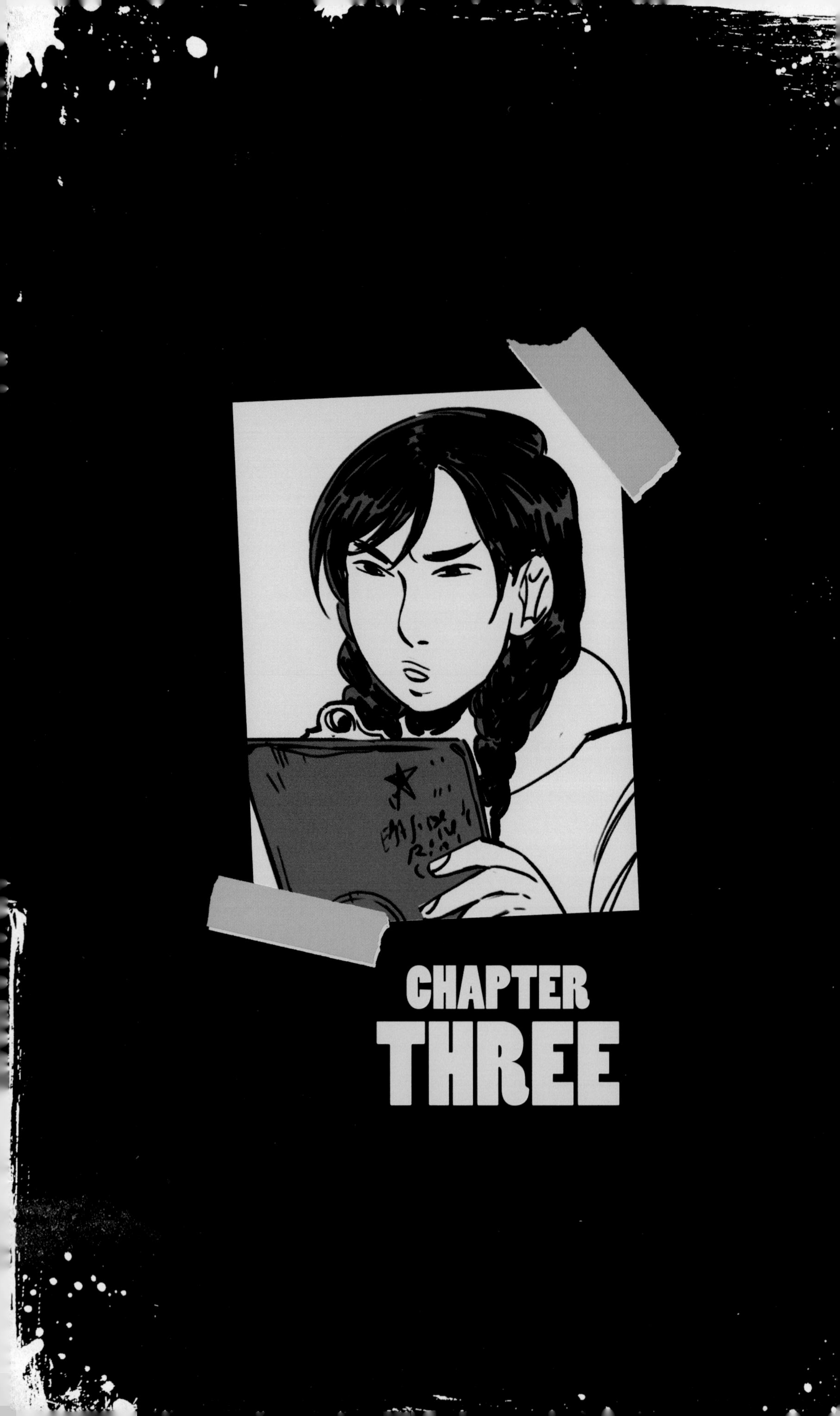
CHAPTER
THREE

FRESH MEAT ROOKIE RUMBLE PRACTICE. PINK AND BLACK SCRIMMAGE.
CALL IT! CALL IT OFF!
CALL OFF THE JAM!
TWEET TWEET TWEET TWEET
YES!
NO!

WHAT'S WRONG? I GOT ALL MY POINTS.
BUT YOU TOOK SO LONG THE OTHER JAMMER GOT TWO.
BUT I GOT FOUR POINTS.
SO DID SHE. DO THE MATH. YOU BOTH GOT FOUR, SO BASICALLY YOU BOTH GOT ZERO.
YOU WEREN'T WATCHING HER, YOU WERE BUSY BEING GREEDY.
DERBY LIFE LESSON #34: SOMETIMES YOU GOTTA CALL IT OFF EARLY.

KRISTEN! JAMMER!
SHE JAMS A LOT. CAN I JAM NEXT?
BUT I--
I'M WORKING FROM LINEUPS I'M TESTING OUT.
SIT.
MAYBE THAT'S WHAT SHE DID TO ME. CALLED IT OFF EARLY.
I KNOW SHE HAS A LOT ON HER MIND.
I GOTTA STOP FIXATING.

TWEET
I AM SO BAD AT THIS PART.
I WASN'T PLANNING ON CONSIDERING HER. WAS I CONSIDERING HER?
WHEN DID SHE START CONSIDERING ME?
UNH!
GETUPGETUP GET UP!
I CAN'T BREATHE!

UOY OKYA? RIKSTEN?
KRISTEN
KRISTEN
HRRK
HRRF
HRRK
RUN! RUN! RUN RUN RUN RUNRUNRUNRUN--

HAS ANYBODY SEEN KRISTEN?
BREATHE.
YOU CAN'T BREATHE.
BREATHE.
YOU CAN'T BREATHE.
YOU'RE DYING.
YOU'RE OKAY YOU'RE OKAY YOU'RE OKAY.

ARE YOU OKAY?
YEAH. JUST FRUSTRATED.
ME TOO.
AND I'M HUNGRY.
YOU'RE ALMOST DONE. BOTH OF YOU.
THIS IS WHO YOUR GRANDDAUGHTER IS NOW. A MEAN COACH.
THE OTHER TEAM? THEY LOVE THEIR COACH.

"THEY WENT TO DISNEYLAND.
"AND AN ESCAPE ROOM.
"THEY EVEN WENT TO THE MUSEUM OF BROKEN RELATIONSHIPS."

"BUT JEN MADE HER TEAM SKATE THE ROSE BOWL IN NINETY-DEGREE HEAT--
"--AND DO THEIR STREET TEAM REQUIREMENT AT THE SAME TIME! SHE'S SO MEAN!"
Rose Bowl
HERE YOU GO! IT'S IN SIX WEEKS.
WE'RE JUST VISITING FROM CHICAGO.

THEY EVEN CALL HER "*TALL MEAN.*"
THEY DO?
I THOUGHT YOU KNEW THAT.
SORRY.
YOUR MOM DID SUCH A GOOD JOB WITH YOU.

WEDNESDAY NIGHT. FRESH MEAT AGILITY WORK AND METEORFIGHTS OFF-SKATES. EXTRA PRIVATE.
JEEZ. AGAIN.
I'LL GET ANOTHER FROM THE OFFICE.
DON'T. THEY'LL JUST TRASH IT.
COMEDY ALERT
FLEXY NOT SEXY
ESRG ★ Aug 7tH
DOORS@6
WHAT'S WITH THE TOOLS?
I'M HELPING THE PIT CREW FIX THE TRACK.
I HAVE TO WAIT HERE FOR MAISIE TO FINISH PRACTICE, ANYWAY, SO I FIGURED WHY NOT?

HERE'S TO THE UNSUNG HEROES OF ROLLER DERBY.
CRUNCH-PIP-PIP-POP
FROM THE ONES WHO FIX US UP...
...TO THE ONES WHO BREAK US DOWN.
EXIT
GOOD SONG.
THEY GET US JUMPING.
ARMS!
THEY MAKE US SIT.

FASTER, FASTER, KILL KILL KILL
THEY CHEER. THEY SCREAM. THEY SHOUT. THEY SHOOT.
THEY WAIT.
THEY WAIT.
10:37
ROLLER DERBY IS A TRUE LABOR OF LOVE. SOMETIMES THE MVP DOESN'T EVEN KNOW HOW TO SKATE.

I'M READY.
'KAY.
SEE YA.
BYE, THEO!
THANKS, MAN.
YEAH, ANYTIME.
DO YOU KNOW WHO KEEPS RIPPING DOWN THE RUMBLE POSTERS?
WELL, I DON'T THINK IT'S *ONE* PERSON. IT'S... *WHY?*
WHAT DO YOU MEAN, *'WHY'?*
JUST... WHY DO YOU WANT TO KNOW?
BECAUSE WE'RE TALKING? I'M HAVING A CONVERSATION WITH YOU.
ARE YOU?

NO. NOT ANYMORE.
DONE TRYING THAT.
IT'S JUST WEIRD, OF ALL THE QUESTIONS TO ASK--
DONE TALKING.
THIS IS HUMILIATING.
IT'S NOT IDEAL.
...FIVE!
SIX!

SATURDAY 9:30AM. PINK TEAM EXTRA EXTRA PRIVATE.
SEVEN!
EIGHT!

AT MY OLD LEAGUE, THIS WOULD HAVE MADE PEOPLE WALK OUT.
BZZT BZZT
WHAT IS WITH YOUR PHONE? IT'S BEEN BLOWING UP.
JUST... SOMEONE.
YOU NOTICE SHE NEVER LETS ME JAM?
Talk to me...I summon you...look at me...
I could make you so happy...the skin on the back of your knee kills me...
I miss you...
BLAH BLAH BLAH MY OLD LEAGUE BLAH

...BUT MY OLD LEAGUE WAS DIFFERENT LIKE THAT.
...I MEAN, IT WAS COMPETITIVE, TOO, BUT HERE IT'S *REALLY* COMPETITIVE.
UH-HUH...
SO YOU AGREE? THAT WE SHOULD SAY SOMETHING TO THE SKATER REP?
UH... WHAT?
IT'S OKAY. YOU HAVE EVERY RIGHT TO SPEAK UP. BEFORE THIS GETS ANY MORE OUT OF HAND.
HUH?
BZZT
BZZT

WELL...
I KNOW. YOU CAN BE HONEST.
THE LITTLE ONES AREN'T FAST ENOUGH AND THE BIG ONES AREN'T LOW ENOUGH. THE ONE WITH THE CRUSH ON YOU IS YOUR BEST JAMMER. BUT YOU KNOW THAT.
WHO?
YOU KNOW THAT, TOO.
YEP, YOU'VE GOT A REAL UNDERDOG STORY BREWING HERE.

GASP
WE'RE GONNA FINISH UP WITH A LITTLE SHOE DERBY, SO PUT ON YOUR GEAR.
I CAN'T. I HAVE TO GO.
EVERYTHING OKAY?

IS SHE OKAY?
NO. WHAT'S WITH THIS POWER PLAY?
HUMILIATING US IN FRONT OF THESE CHILDREN. THEY'RE NOT BUYING TICKETS.
THE OTHER TEAM IS GOING TO AN ICE CREAM PARTY TONIGHT WHILE I'M SOAKING IN EPSOM SALTS.
GOOD. THAT TEAM WILL BE BETTER AT EATING ICE CREAM. YOURS WILL BE BETTER AT ROLLER DERBY.
I'M A ROLLER BIRDIE.
ROLLER BURBEES!
AND YEAH, THESE GIRLS CAN'T PAY TO SEE YOU. BUT MAYBE ONE DAY THEY'LL WANT TO BE YOU.
SO DO ME A FAVOR: SHUT UP AND GEAR UP. BE A ROLE MODEL.

GET ENOUGH STUFF FOR THREE DAYS.
THREE? I PROBABLY JUST NEED TO STAY THE NIGHT.
YOU NEED TO REPORT THIS. A RESTRAINING ORDER. SOMETHING.
NO, IT'LL JUST MAKE IT WORSE. AND PLEASE DON'T TELL MOM.

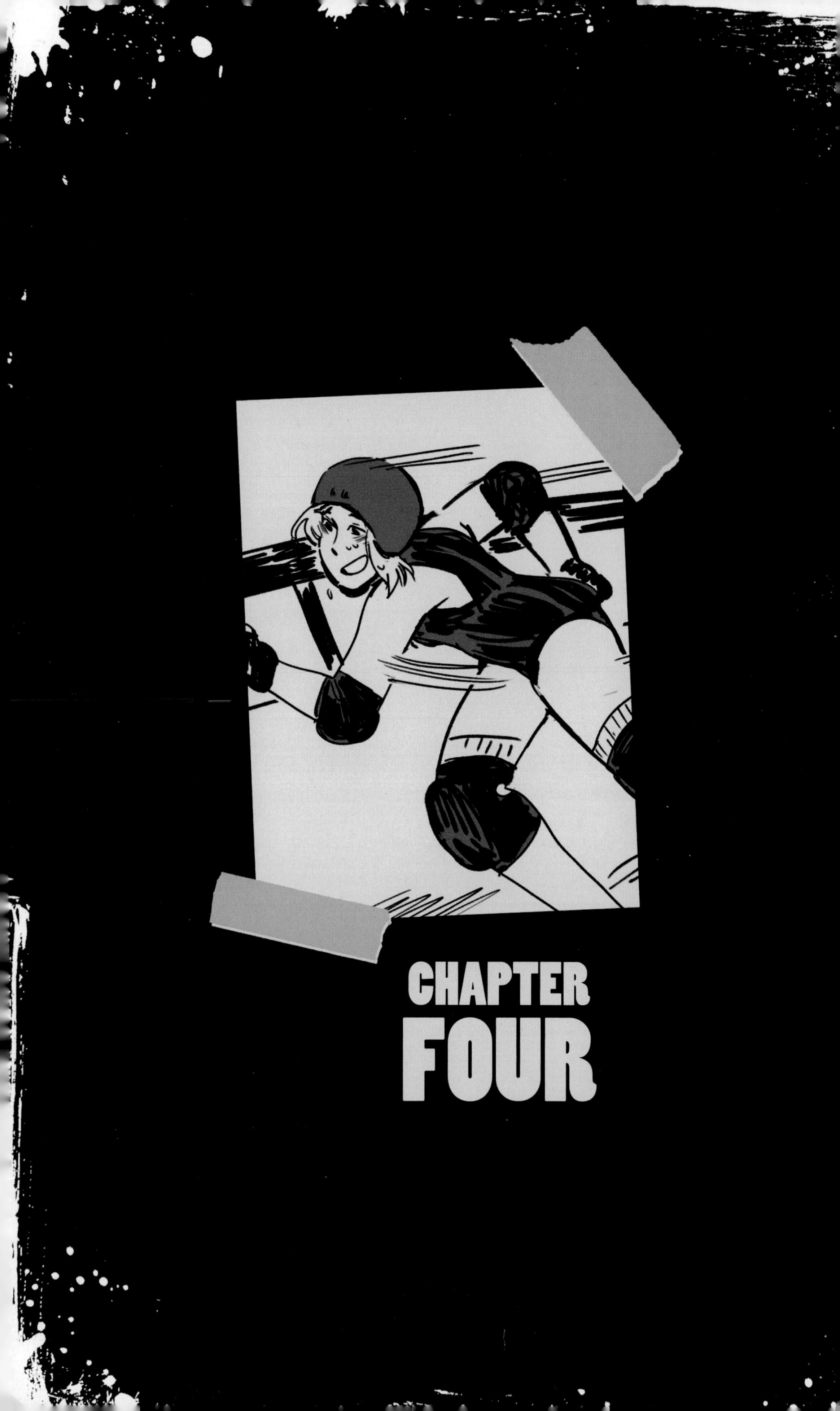

CHAPTER FOUR

"HEY!"

WHEN ARE YOU GONNA DEAL WITH ME?
KRISTEN
KNOCKOUT

COME ON. GET UP, LAZYFACE.
WHA... LÃOLAO?
MOM JUST LET YOU INTO MY APARTMENT?
HOW LONG HAVE YOU BEEN HERE? YOU CLEANED.
ONLY THE LOW PARTS.
I COULD SUE YOUR BUILDING.
PLEASE DON'T CAUSE TROUBLE.
YOU'VE GOT CLOTHES THAT NEED TO GO IN THE DRYER. TALL PERSON'S JOB.
COME ON. WE'VE GOT A BIG DAY.

I HADN'T REALIZED HOW MUCH OF MY STUFF HAD KINDA DRIFTED OVER HERE.
I TOTALLY DON'T MIND.
I CAN'T BELIEVE YOU'LL BE GONE FOR THREE DAYS.
I KNOW. IT'S THE LONGEST WE'VE EVER BEEN APART.
ARE YOU SURE YOU'LL BE OKAY? YOUR ARM...
AW. YOU NOTICED.
YES. DON'T WORRY ABOUT ME. HAVE FUN WITH THE TRACK RATS.*
*TRACK RATS: THE VOLUNTEERS WHO FIX THE DERBY TRACK.

I'LL TEXT YOU WHEN WE GET TO VEGAS.
SHUT
=SNIFF=
NAKED ALONE TIME!
TOO MANY SNACKS AND BINGEING PROJECT RUNWAY TIME!
READING IN THE TUB UNTIL EVERYTHING IS COLD TIME!
SAD BUT SUPER SOFT PJs TIME!
...CAN'T FALL ASLEEP UNTIL I SNIFF HIS PILLOW TIME.
=SNNNIFFFFFF=

SATURDAY MORNING. PINK AND BLACK ROOKIE RUMBLE SCRIMMAGE.
HOME OF THE EASTSIDE ROLLER GIRLS
TIME OUT! TWO MINUTE TIME OUT.
WE'RE GETTING KILLED OUT THERE!
STICK TOGETHER! ALWAYS HAVE A PARTNER!
THEY'RE KNOCKING YOU DOWN BECAUSE YOU'RE ALONE!
WHERE THE CRAP IS KRISTEN?
I DON'T KNOW. SHE MISSED YESTERDAY, TOO.
RED KENNEDY
CHERRY BOMB

AT MY LAST LEAGUE, THEY NEVER MADE US PRACTICE THIS EARLY ON A SATURDAY.
BOMBER, YOU JAM NEXT.
THANKS.

WAIT UNTIL WE GET IN THE CAR.
YOUR TEAM IS A MESS.
THEY'RE NOT HAVING ANY FUN. THEY AREN'T SEEING ANY RESULTS. THEIR BEST PLAYER ISN'T EVEN SHOWING UP. WHY SHOULD *THEY?*
I CAN'T BELIEVE YOU'RE TAKING THEIR SIDE.
A TEAM ONLY HAS ONE SIDE.
IT *IS* THE SIDE.
THEY'VE ALREADY GOT A GREAT COACH. NOW THEY NEED A GREAT LEADER.

DO YOU LIKE IT?
ROOKIE RUMBLE
WHAT IS THIS FOR?
I'M PRESENTING IT TO THE ART DEPARTMENT.
I CAME UP WITH IT ON THE DRIVE HOME FROM VEGAS.
HOW'S YOUR ARM?
FINE. I DON'T NEED THE SLING ANYMORE.
THAT'S GREAT!

SO, IS THIS YOUR THING, NOW?
WHAT?
DERBY. IS THIS YOUR THING?
WELL, I MEAN, I'VE YET TO SCRIMMAGE, BUT THE PUSHY RIOTS HAVE BEEN ASKING WHEN I AM THINKING ABOUT GETTING TRACK CLEARED FOR FRESH MEAT.
MAISIE, I AM AT THAT TRACK BECAUSE OF YOU.

WELL, THAT'S... I DIDN'T ASK YOU TO.
I *KNOW.* I *LIKE* BEING THERE. I'M NOT TRYING TO CO-OPT ANYTHING. THIS ISN'T FAIR.
IT'S JUST... I... I HAD NOTHING WHEN I FOUND DERBY. IT WASN'T SUPPOSED TO HAVE A BOYFRIEND IN IT, THAT WAS KIND OF THE POINT.
FINE. YOU WANT ME TO STOP GOING?
NO. YES. *NO.* I DON'T KNOW. I FEEL WEIRD.
WHERE SHOULD WE FIGHT NEXT?
DEFINITELY THE BATHROOM.

CAN CAN
HFFFT
DINK
0:00:01
LAP 1
LAP 2
RESET

NO! NOT MY SHOULDER!

YOU OKAY?
OWWWWW. YEAH. THANKS. OOOH.
NICE WORK IN THERE.
WAS THAT GAL TALKING TO YOU?
YEAH. I GUESS I SCARE HER LESS WHEN I'M SKATING.
YOU GOT AN HOUR? I COULD USE SOME HELP WITH MY BITTER, SAD TEAM.
SURE. BUT I HAVE TO GO WHEN THEO IS DONE WITH THE ART DEPARTMENT MEETING.
WE ARE ON DAY THREE OF A FIGHT AND WE'RE ALMOST DONE RE-ORGANIZING THE PANTRY.

THERE'S KRISTEN. I NEED TO TALK TO HER.
WARM THEM UP FOR ME, WOULD YOU?
SURE THING.
WHAT'S GOING ON?
I'M SORRY. I'M NOT GOING TO WAIT ON MY BROTHER TO DRIVE ME ANYMORE. HE'S UNRELIABLE. I'LL JUST USE MY CAR.
YOU HAVE A CAR?!
YEAH, I DON'T LIKE TO USE IT, BUT I HATE MISSING PRACTICES.

DO YOU WANT TO TALK ABOUT WHAT'S GOING ON?
ONLY IF YOU MEAN BETWEEN US.
KRISTEN
IMPRESSIVE CHANGE OF SUBJECT.
LOOK. I LIKE TO COMPARTMENTALIZE. I AM A HUMAN BENTO BOX.
WHEN I'M AT DERBY, I'M ALL DERBY. THERE'S ONLY NOW. NO PAST.
AND THIS OTHER STUFF, IT'S NOT ABOUT DERBY. AND IT'S NOT ABOUT YOU. SO DON'T WORRY ABOUT IT.
BUT AS FOR *YOU*...

I WANT TO CALL YOU JENNIFER.
KRISTEN
XXX 666
I... I WAS GOING TO ASK YOU TO... BE CAPTAIN.
AND I AM ASKING YOU TO GO ON A DATE WITH ME. WHERE I CALL YOU JENNIFER.

WHY DO YOU KEEP SAYING MY NAME LIKE THAT?
KRISTEN
BECAUSE IT'S HOW I HEAR IT IN MY HEAD.
ALL THE TIME.
...JENNIFER...
JUST...SAY YOU'LL BE MY CAPTAIN.
I WILL. IF YOU GO ON A DATE WITH ME.
THIS IS EMOTIONAL BLACKMAIL.
DO YOU LIKE IT?

COME ON, LADIES! BUTTS IN THE AIR ON THESE BEAR CRAWLS! YOU CAN DO IT!
I'M STAYING TO HELP KNOCKOUT.
OKAY, GREAT. I JUST WANTED TO TELL YOU--MY POSTER. THEY LOVED IT. IT'S GOING UP TOMORROW.
THAT'S... GREAT. CONGRATULATIONS.
I MADE SOME CHANGES.
ROOKIE RUMBLE
THIS IS HER STORY

PINK TEAM, LISTEN UP! I'M SORRY I'VE BEEN GONE.
I'M NOT GOING TO GIVE YOU AN EXCUSE OR REASON BECAUSE YOU'RE BETTER THAN THAT.
KRISTEN
WHEN I'M ON THIS TRACK, WHEN I'M ON YOUR TEAM, YOU'RE GOING TO GET THE BEST OF ME.
OFF THE TRACK, SOMEONE ELSE WILL GET ALL THIS HOTNESS, BUT THAT'S NONE OF YOUR BUSINESS.
SO FROM THIS MOMENT UNTIL WE HEAR THAT LAST WHISTLE OF OUR ROOKIE RUMBLE, LET'S MAKE A PROMISE.
LET'S GIVE THE BEST OF OURSELVES TO EACH OTHER. STAY STRONG AND *WIN THIS THING!*
KRISTEN

HANDS IN!
PINK TEAM!
LET'S GO!
...WE REALLY NEED A NAME...
PACK IT UP!
STICK TOGETHER!
MOVE YOUR FEET!
YOU GOT THIS!
DERBY LIFE LESSON #44:
NOBODY SKATES ALONE.
THE END

ISSUE #1 MAIN COVER BY
VERONICA FISH

ISSUE #1 SUBSCRIPTION COVER BY
JEN BARTEL

ISSUE #2 MAIN COVER BY
VERONICA FISH

ISSUE #2 SUBSCRIPTION COVER BY
MEREDITH GRAN
WITH COLORS BY BRITTANY PEER

ISSUE #3 MAIN COVER BY
VERONICA FISH
VF

ISSUE #3 SUBSCRIPTION COVER BY
JEN BARTEL

JEN
BAR
TEL

ISSUE #4 MAIN COVER BY
VERONICA FISH

ISSUE #4 SUBSCRIPTION COVER BY
KAT LEYH

CHARACTER DESIGNS BY
VERONICA FISH